A Note to Parents and Caregivers:

Read-it! Readers are for children who are just starting on the amazing road to reading. These beautiful books support both the acquisition of reading skills and the love of books.

The RED LEVEL presents familiar topics using common words and repeating sentence patterns.

The BLUE LEVEL presents new ideas using a larger vocabulary and varied sentence structure.

The YELLOW LEVEL presents more challenging ideas, a broad vocabulary, and wide variety in sentence structure.

The GREEN LEVEL presents more complex ideas, an extended vocabulary range, and expanded language structures.

When sharing a book with your child, read in short stretches, pausing often to talk about the pictures. Have your child turn the pages and point to the pictures and familiar words. And be sure to reread favorite stories or parts of stories.

There is no right or wrong way to share books with children. Find time to read with your child, and pass on the legacy of literacy.

Adria F. Klein, Ph.D.
Professor Emeritus
California State University
San Bernardino, California

Editor: Bob Temple
Creative Director: Terri Foley
Editorial Adviser: Andrea Cascardi
Copy Editor: Laurie Kahn
Designer: Melissa Voda
Page production: The Design Lab
The illustrations in this book were painted with watercolor.

Picture Window Books
5115 Excelsior Boulevard
Suite 232
Minneapolis, MN 55416
1-877-845-8392
www.picturewindowbooks.com

Printed in the United States of America.

Library of Congress Cataloging-in-Publication Data
White, Mark, 1971–
The ant and the grasshopper : a retelling of Aesop's fable / written
by Mark White ; illustrated by Sara Rojo.
p. cm. — (Read-it! readers fairy tales)
Summary: Retells the fable about an industrious ant that busily prepares for
the approaching winter while a grasshopper makes no plans for the cold weather to come.
ISBN 1-4048-0217-7
[1. Folklore. 2. Fables.] I. Aesop. II. Rojo, Sara, 1973– ill. III. Title. IV. Series.
PZ8.2.W55An 2004
398.24'525726 21—dcaE   2003006302

Read-it! Readers
Yellow Level

The Ant and the Grasshopper

A Retelling of Aesop's Fable

Written by Mark White

Illustrated by Sara Rojo

Library Adviser:
Kathy Baxter, M.A.
Former Coordinator of Children's Services
Anoka County (Minnesota) Library

Reading Advisers:
Adria F. Klein, Ph.D.
Professor Emeritus, California State University
San Bernardino, California

Susan Kesselring, M.A.
Literacy Educator
Rosemount-Apple Valley-Eagan (Minnesota) School District

Picture Window Books
Minneapolis, Minnesota

An ant once lived
next to a grasshopper
in a large field.

The ant woke early
each summer morning.
He was a serious worker.

From sunrise until sunset,
the ant harvested food.
He stored it in his home.

Every morning, the grasshopper
woke up singing.

The grasshopper had a nice voice.
He loved to make music. All day long,
he sang and danced.

9

"Come sing with me,"
the grasshopper said
every time he saw the ant.

"I can't stop now," the ant always said.

"Not even for one song?"
the grasshopper begged.
"It's such a lovely day!"

But the ant kept working.

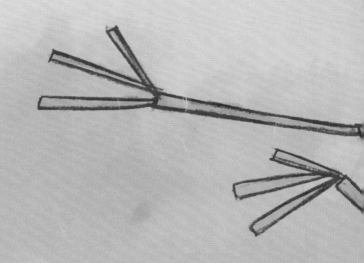

13

On rainy days,
the grasshopper stayed at home.
He made up new songs
to keep from being bored.

The ant worked at home,
storing his food for winter.

One winter day, the grasshopper
went outside to look for food.
He found nothing to eat.

The grasshopper knocked
on his neighbor's door.
He asked for some food.

19

"You spent all summer singing while I worked," the ant said.

"Now you can spend the winter
dancing to keep warm."

"But you have food stored,"
the grasshopper said.

"That's because I spent the summer getting ready for winter," the ant replied.

23

"There's a time for play
and a time for work," the ant said.

24